ZPL

W9-BGI-515

USBORNE FIRST READING
Level Three

WITHDRAWN

USBORNE FIRST READING

The **Dinosaur**
Who Lost His **ROAR**

Russell Punter
Illustrated by Andy Elkerton

USBORNE FIRST READING

The **Castle**
That **Jack Built**

Lesley Sims
Illustrated by
Mike Gordon

USBORNE FIRST READING

**Chicken
Licken**

retold by
Russell Punter
Illustrated by Ann Kronheimer

USBORNE FIRST READING

The **Three Little
Pigs**

retold by
Susanna Davidson
Illustrated by Georgien Overwater

The Three Little Pigs

Retold by
Susanna Davidson

Illustrated by
Georgien Overwater

Reading Consultant: Alison Kelly
Roehampton University

Once upon a time, there were three little pigs...

Pinky,

Percy

and

Poppy.

They lived with their
mother in a pretty
little house.

But the little pigs grew
too big.

"We want homes of our own," they said.

Build strong, safe houses!

So they packed their bags and waved goodbye.

"Watch out for the
Big Bad Wolf," called
Mother Pig.

The three little pigs
trotted along until...

...they met a man
selling straw.

"Can I buy some straw?"
asked Pinky Pig.

"I'm going to build
a house."

11

Pinky Pig worked
very fast. He made
four straw walls

a straw roof and a
straw door.

Then he put down a
soft straw floor.

"Look at my house!"
he said. "Isn't it grand?"

I *am* a
clever pig.

Then he went inside
and shut the door.

Percy and Poppy Pig
trotted on until...

Sticks
for
sale

...they met a man selling sticks.
"Can I buy some sticks?" asked Percy Pig.

I'm going to build a house.

"Sticks are better than straw."

19

Then he went inside and shut the door.

Poppy Pig trotted on until...

...she saw some bricks
for sale.

"Can I buy some bricks?"
asked Poppy Pig.

Bricks
for sale

"I'm going to build
a house."

Poppy Pig worked hard.

"Bricks are better than straw," she said.

"Bricks are better
than sticks."

"But they're so heavy."

25

At last, the brick house was finished.

The next day, the Big
Bad Wolf went to the
straw house.

"Little pig, little pig, let me come in," he called.

"No!" cried Pinky Pig. "Not by the hair on my chinny-chin-chin."

"Then I'll huff and I'll
puff and I'll blow your
house in," said the wolf.

30

And he huffed
and he puffed

and he blew the house in.

Pinky ran as fast as he could to the stick house.

The wolf was just behind him.

"Little pigs, little pigs,
let me come in," said
the wolf.

"No!" cried Percy Pig.
"Not by the hair on my
chinny-chin-chin."

34

"Then I'll huff and I'll puff and I'll blow your house in," said the wolf.

And he huffed
and he puffed

and he huffed
and he puffed

36

until at last he blew
the house in.

Pinky and Percy ran
as fast as they could
to the brick house.

The wolf was just
behind them.

"Little pigs, little pigs, let me come in," said the wolf.

"No!" cried Poppy Pig.
"Not by the hair on my
chinny-chin-chin."

"Then I'll huff and I'll puff and I'll bloW your house in," said the wolf.

And he huffed and he
puffed and he huffed

and he puffed. He huffed and puffed until...

...he ran out of puff.
"Hee, hee, hee," laughed
the three little pigs.

"I'm coming to get you!"
cried the wolf.

He jumped onto the roof.

He slid down
the chimney

and landed *splosh*
in Poppy's cooking pot.

The three little pigs
slammed on the lid.

And that was the end of
the Big Bad Wolf.

The Three Little Pigs is a very old story. It was first written down around two hundred years ago, but people were telling it to each other long before then.

Series editor: Lesley Sims

Designed by Louise Flutter

First published in 2007 by Usborne Publishing Ltd., Usborne House, 83-85 Saffron Hill, London EC1N 8RT, England. www.usborne.com
Copyright © 2007 Usborne Publishing Ltd.

USBORNE FIRST READING
Level Four

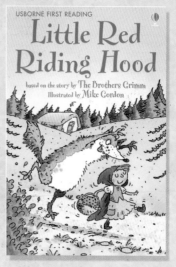